Beverly Billingsly Takes the Cake

ALEXANDER STADLER

GULLIVER BOOKS

HARCOURT, INC.

Orlando   Austin   New York   San Diego   Toronto   London

www.HarcourtBooks.com

Library of Congress Cataloging-in-Publication Data
Stadler, Alexander.
Beverly Billingsly takes the cake/Alexander Stadler.
p. cm.
Summary: Beverly runs into a problem while making the "caramel candy castle cake"
for Oliver's party, but her creativity and her mother's encouragement save the day.
[1. Cake—Fiction. 2. Baking—Fiction. 3. Creative ability—Fiction.
4. Imagination—Fiction. 5. Parties—Fiction.] I. Title.
PZ7.S77573Bh 2005
[E]—dc22   2004004171
ISBN 0-15-205357-3
First edition
A C E G H F D B

Manufactured in China

The illustrations in this book were done in gouache and ink on Bristol Board.
The display type was set in Barcelona.
The text type was set in Bell.
Color separations by Colourscan Co. Pte. Ltd., Singapore
Manufactured by South China Printing Company, Ltd., China
This book was printed on totally chlorine-free Stora Enso Matte paper.
Production supervision by Wendi Taylor
Designed by Lydia D'moch

This book was inspired by my mother,
who always said, "Make it a flower."

To Peter Cohen, for a start
—A. S.

Beverly Billingsly said that she would bake the cake herself.

"All of the other children will be buying presents or making cards for Oliver," she thought. "But the most important part of any party is the cake. That's the grand finale. And I know just which one I want to make, too."

Beverly ran to her bookshelf and came back with a well-worn copy of *Louella Millbank's Book of Incredible Desserts.*

In the middle of the chapter on cake was a picture Beverly had been staring at for years.

"It's called the Caramel Candy Castle Cake," she told Mrs. Billingsly. "I think that it is one of the most beautiful things I have ever seen."

"It looks a little complicated," said Mrs. Billingsly.

"No, it's easy," said Beverly. "All you need are four ice-cream cones, a package of wafer cookies, two round layers of butterscotch cake, frosting, and three bags of the candy of your choice. Then you just assemble it according to the directions."

For Beverly, looking at the picture of the cake was like stepping into a magical world.

"I just know that Oliver is going to love it!" Beverly
told her mother.

"Let's bake it the day before the party," said Mrs. Billingsly.
"A cake always tastes better when it's had a day to rest."

For a week, Beverly's mind was fixed
on the Caramel Candy Castle Cake.

She dreamt about it in bed,

at the dinner table,

and even in the tub.

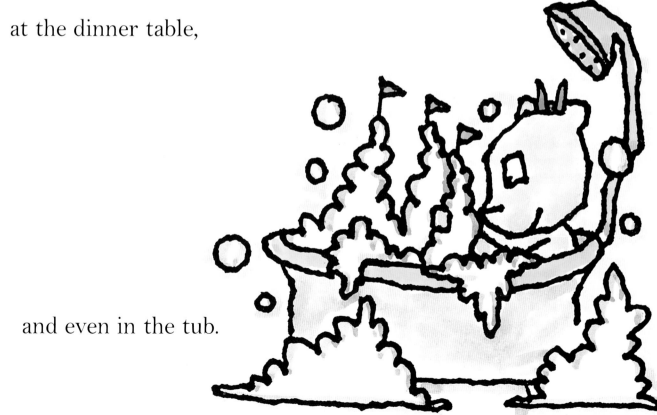

A few days before the party, Beverly and her father
went to the grocery store to buy the ingredients. Beverly
skipped through the market as she checked off the items
on her list. It took her forty-five minutes to select the
candy of her choice.

"What have you been doing here all this time?" asked Mr. Billingsly.

"Choosing the perfect candy," answered Beverly.

Beverly woke up early on baking day to set everything
they needed on the kitchen counter.

Beverly and her mother preheated
the oven and prepared the batter.

Then the phone rang. "I'll be back in just a minute, Beverly," said Mrs. Billingsly. It was Aunt Bethesda, calling from a tent in the Kalahari.

Beverly couldn't wait. She poured the batter into the pan.

When her mother returned, they put the cake into the oven and set the timer.

It took an hour and a half for the cake to bake and cool.
To Beverly, it felt like an eternity.

When the cake was finally ready, Mrs. Billingsly flipped the pan over to release it. It didn't budge. "It seems to be stuck," she said.

Beverly's eyes grew wide with panic. While her mother was on the phone, she had skipped step number seven: "Grease the pan."

"Honey, are you all right?" asked Mrs Billingsly. "You don't look so good. . . . This cake is really stuck," she murmured. "I think we're going to have to cut it in half to get it out."

"I've ruined everything!" cried Beverly. She ran to her room and slammed the door.

"My cake is WRECKED! RUINED! DESTROYED!" shouted Beverly as she punched her pillow. "Now I'll have nothing to give Oliver!" And then she collapsed onto the floor.

A few minutes later, there was a knock at her door.
"Beverly," said Mrs. Billingsly, "why don't you come take
another look at the cake and we'll see what we can do."

"Remember when you spilled the paint on your book report and then you turned the stain into a flower? asked Mrs. Billingsly.

"Yes," answered Beverly.

"Well, I want you to think about that and tell me if this looks like anything you've seen before."

Beverly took a deep breath and opened her eyes.

"It doesn't look like a castle, that's for sure," said Beverly.

"Look again," said Mrs Billingsly. "It must look like something."

Beverly's eyes lit up and she smiled.

Beverly picked up the frosting and the candy. In less
than an hour she was looking at the most beautiful
butterfly cake she had ever seen.

"She needs antennae." Beverly said. She ran and got
some pipe cleaners from her craft corner.

Oliver was fascinated by the cake. "I think that it is one of the most beautiful things I have ever seen," he said.

Carlton Chlomsky couldn't stop looking at it. "Do you think you could make an evil dragon cake for my birthday in November?" he asked.

As Beverly was walking home, she wondered whether—
along with becoming a paleontologist and a famous actor—
she might want to be a pastry chef, as well.